Where Are You, Hashem?

by YAFFA GANZ

Illustrated by Liat Benyaminy Ariel

4401 Second Avenue / Brooklyn, N.Y. 11232 / (718) 921-9000
Produced by SEFERCRAFT, INC. / Brooklyn, N.Y.

Hello, Hashem! I looked for You the other day inside my Daddy's *shul* – the one he learns and *davens* in. I saw books and benches and tables and chairs and the big *aron kodesh* with all the *Sifrey Torah.*

But I didn't see You. I was so sure You would be there. Where were You, Hashem?

Every morning, Mr. Rafael picks us up in the big yellow school bus and drives us to school. He always says, "Hashem is right here in the bus, driving along with us and keeping us safe."

But where do You sit?
Do you have a special seat
next to Mr. Rafael?

I think You must be somewhere in our school because each day, when we *daven,* our teacher says, "Hashem is listening."

Last week I looked for You all over the building, but I couldn't find You anywhere.

א
י ט ח ז ו ה
צ פ ע ס כ
ת ש

Mommy said our new baby was a gift from You. I didn't see You bring him into the house when Mommy came home from the hospital. I didn't see You at the *bris* either. But Daddy said You were right there, looking after the baby. How come I couldn't see You?

Daddy says, "Hashem is the world's best doctor." He says You can cure anyone, no matter how sick he is. When we visited Aunt Nomi in Mt. Sinai hospital, I was sure I'd find You there. I saw lots of doctors and lots of nurses, but I didn't see You. Do You work in a different hospital?

You must be very rich because You give so many people food to eat and clothes to wear and houses to live in. I bet you own a bank!

Once, I looked for You in Mommy's bank, but I couldn't find You. Were You down in the vault? The guard wouldn't let me go down there to look.

BAN

I thought I might find You in the supermarket since You're the One who makes our food grow. I pushed a wagon through all the aisles and I searched on all the shelves. I found lots of food, but I didn't find You.

1.9

Uncle Yossi is an
artist. He draws
beautiful pictures.
He told me, "Hashem
guides my hands
and helps me
in my work."

I looked for You
in Uncle Yossi's studio,
but I couldn't find You.

I know You made all the animals in the zoo, and You did a great job, especially with the elephants!

I was sure You must be the Director. But when we passed the Director's office, someone else was sitting there. Is Your office downtown?

Once I saw an empty swing in the park moving back and forth, all by itself. For a minute, I thought maybe You were swinging on it! But I suppose it was just the wind. Do You ever swing? It's lots of fun.

I know You created
the land and the sky and the sea.
Are You somewhere up above the clouds?
Or maybe deep down inside the water?

Bubby said that Eretz Yisrael is Your Holy Land and Yerushalayim is Your Holy City. She said that even though Your Holy Temple – the *Beis Hamikdash* – was destroyed a long time ago, You never left the Land or the City.

I looked at Bubby's pictures of Jerusalem, and I saw lots of buildings and streets. I was wondering ... which part of the city do You live in nowadays?

On *Erev Shabbos,* when Mommy lights the candles, I always look for You. I know You must be in our house somewhere! I wonder if You are hidden inside the flames . . .

My friend Meir said You can't be in *our* house on *Shabbos* because that's when You're in *his* house. When I said You're in our house too, Meir wanted to know how You can be in two places at once. I discussed it with Mommy and now I think I know the answer . . .

Even though no one can *ever* see You,

You are always
EVERYWHERE!

אַיֵּה מְקוֹם כְּבוֹדוֹ?
כְּבוֹדוֹ מָלֵא עוֹלָם!

Where can Hashem be found?
His glory fills the entire world!

Good Middos are the good traits the Torah tells us about – traits which help make us better Jews and better people. If we have good *middos,* we will always act, and say, and do things in the proper way.

But where can we find good *middos*? No one sells them or gives them away. We can only acquire them by looking and learning, by watching and listening. And by practicing.

In the **ArtScroll Middos Books**, you will find lots of interesting, exciting, fun-to-read stories with beautiful pictures. Each story will help you learn something new and important about **good middos.**

Enjoy!